KU-473-942

This Wee Book Belongs to

....

....

To a muse – wherever it come from

To my daughter, whose idea was the
muse and for my other children who were
dragged to many a poetry night as I
learned my craft.

Santa's Adventure at Loch Ness
First published in Great Britain in 2022
Paperback ISBN 978-1-7396790-7-1

Text Copyright © Sam Steele
Illustration Copyright © Sarah-Leigh Wills

Sam Steele and Sarah-Leigh Wills have asserted their right to be identified as the author and
Illustrator of this Work in accordance with the Copyright, Designs and Patents Act 1988. All rights reserved.
No part of this publication may be reproduced, stored in a retrieval system, transmitted, or copied in any form
or by any means, electronic, mechanical, photocopying, recording or otherwise, without the prior written permission
of the publisher and copyright owner.

Illustration and Design by:
www.happydesigner.co.uk

Santa's Adventure at Loch Ness

By Sam Steele

Doodled by Sarah-Leigh Wills

T'was the night before Christmas, all bairns in their beds
And jolly old Santa was aboot on his sled

With a bag full of treasures, he delivers himself
To give a wee rest to the hard-working elves

He didn't need Rudolph, 'cos the forecast was clear
As he sailed past Glenfinnan he was full of good cheer

He then took a left at a rather big Ben
And steered his great sleigh away up the Great Glen

But then, out of nowhere, it appeared in a hurry
T'was lashings of snow in an almighty flurry

Poor Santa was caught with no Rudolph to steer
He got tumbled and tossed and began to feel queer

Adrift in the storm all confused and in doubt
He thought he should stop lest the reindeer gave out

He spied a big loch with a light at the end
And he passed an old castle as he tried to descend

But as he got close, he thought he wouldn't reach
The safety he sought up ahead on the beach

Then at the last second, a few feet from the shore
He bounced off the top of a wee dinosaur

He landed on land, just a thin strip of shingle
From an Inn came the sound of a sweet Christmas jingle

From all of the shoogling Santa felt peelie-wally
It took him a while to return to his jolly

"I thank you" said Santa "You saved me and my sleigh
And all of the presents on this special day"

"But we're lost and we're hungry and need a good guide
To deliver these gifts throughout this countryside"

"Don't worry, I'm Nessie there's no need to despair
It's not often I stick my head up in the air"

"I popped out this day, 'cos it's usually quiet
Sweet tunes from the Inn. If you can, you should try it"

"You're lucky, up here we've the finest of heathers
Tell the reindeer to feast as I have a wee blether"

It was hard to see food through the snow and the sleet
But the coos in the field helped the reindeer to eat

Then Nessie came back with a big bag going clink
And suggested they all drink a bright orange drink

"When the wind is this windy
you need more than thick coats
You need shortbread and tablet
and warm porridge oats"

"We have treats here a plenty and all that we ask
Is that you dine on enough to finish your task"

When all had their fill Nessie started to speak
"I know that the weather is nasty and dreich"

"In the land of the Scots you'll nay have to grieve
'Cos Nessie and pals will help save Christmas eve"

In the Inn I found Eilidh, a sweet unicorn
She'll magically lead with her glittering horn

"She'll stand with the reindeer at the front of the sleigh
And guide you through glens, weather baltic or nay"

When all were tied in and prepared to progress
Eilidh dipped down her head
till her horn touched the Ness

In the proud Highland home of the tartan clad jocks
Is the deepest of waters and a mystical loch

As the horn touched the surface it started to glow
The eight reindeer and Eilidh were ready to go

But the sleigh would not budge, so how could they leave?
For the toys to get going they needed a heave

A wee clan of haggis then started to yelp
They did a big jig now that they too could help

With a push and a shove, it was not long before
The reindeer and Santa to the heavens did soar

Nessie just smiled and waved a big Celtic wave
Then returned to the deep knowing Christmas was saved

The Scots like their haggis and a big hairy coo
They like shortbread and heather,
they like orange drink too

They like tablet and Nessie and now you know why
With a big bowl of porridge, they all helped Santa fly

Glossary

Aboot	About
Bairns	Small children
Baltic	Freezing cold
Ben	Large hill
Blether	Chat
Celtic	Culture of the people of Scotland, Wales, Ireland
Clan	Family group
Coos	Cows
Dreich	Dreary and bleak
Eilidh	Pronounced 'Ay-Lee', a name which translate from Gaelic as 'Radiant'
Glen	Valley
Great Glen	A valley stretching from Inverness (east coast) to Fort William (west coast)
Haggis	Small creature, native only to Scotland
Jig	Dance, as in Jigs and Reels
Loch	Lake
Nay	No
Peelie-wally	Pale and sickly
Shoogling	Shaky, giddy, unsteady
Tablet	A sweet Scottish treat, akin to fudge but more crumbly
Wee	Small